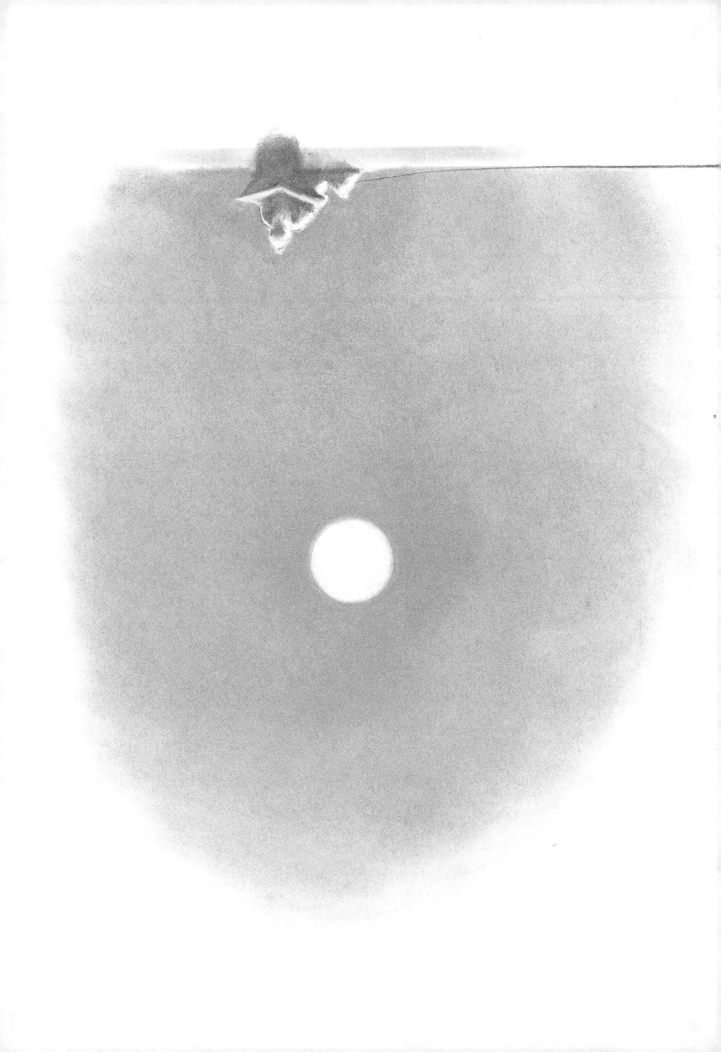

And so it happened that one day the story was told to the governor of Songcheng, who went himself to the inn where Wei Gu had first heard of the matchmaker. And he called this place "The Matrimony Inn," and the temple he called "The Place of Red Thread."

After this day the couple grew even closer. Some time later, to their joy, they had a son. The boy grew up with his family. Years passed and Wei died. The boy, now a man, became governor of Yanmen province. This was such an honor that his mother received a title herself from the emperor of all China.

Now it was Wei's turn to tell his story. When he was done, he said to her, "It is a wonder, isn't it, that our lives and our fortune are known so well in heaven."

Wei could hardly believe what he was hearing. "Was Chen a half-blind woman?" he asked. "Yes," his wife said, "but how did you know?"

"Then one day, while I was on Chen's back, a crazy man stabbed me, leaving this ugly scar on my forehead forever. After two years with Chen, we found my uncle the governor, who took me in as his daughter."

Wei listened to his wife tell her story. She told him that she had been only three years old at that time, and that her wet nurse, a poor farmer named Chen who lived outside of Songcheng, had taken care of her. Each day Chen would bring the baby to market with her so that she could make a little money selling her vegetables.

"What is beneath the flower seed, my dear one?" he asked her.

His good wife broke into tears. "My husband, I am not the daughter of the governor, as you have thought," she cried. "My real father was a guard in the army and died while he was working in Songcheng long ago. My mother and brother also died, one after the other, and I became an orphan."

It was soon after their marriage that Wei noticed his wife always wore a beautiful flower seed between her eyebrows. Even when she was washing or sleeping, she wore it. The flower seed made her look all the more lovely, so Wei thought nothing of it. Then one day he remembered what happened in the market at Songcheng. It had been exactly fourteen years before. Wei went to his wife.

At last Wei had a good wife, and someday he would have a family of his own. Wei was a very happy man.

Finally, because of his father's honorable position, he got a position as a judge in Xiangzhou. There he worked for the governor who appreciated Wei's many talents and his dedication so much that he married his kind and beautiful daughter to Wei.

The same day, Wei promised ten thousand coins to his servant if he would kill the girl. The poor man agreed and Wei went with him to the marketplace and pointed out the girl.

The following morning the servant crept up to the vegetable stall, stabbed the child, then escaped through the marketplace without being caught.

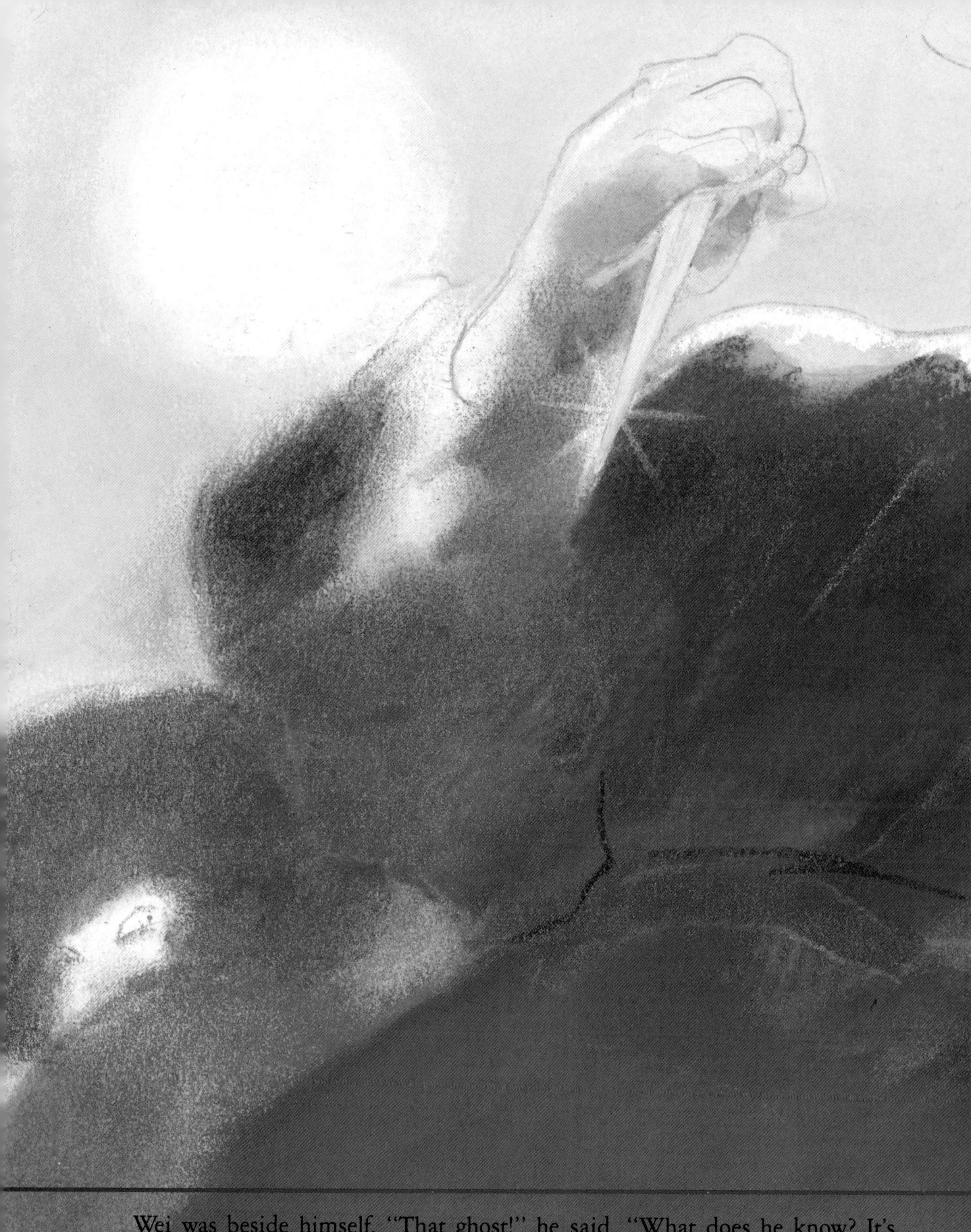

Wei was beside himself. "That ghost!" he said. "What does he know? It's ridiculous! I'm from a good family. But even if I cannot find a wife from a good family, I will never accept such an ugly girl."

"Not so," said the old man. "It is said in my book that she will live a long and happy life, and that someday she will have a fine title because of her own son. No one can change that."

When Wei turned around to argue this, the old man had disappeared.

"That baby will be your wife," the old man whispered.
Wei just stared. A vegetable-monger for a mother! And the baby was ugly!
"I won't marry her!" Wei said in a rage.

By now the sun was rising in the sky, so Wei and the matchmaker went to see at once. There, at the market, in front of a vegetable stall, the old man pointed to a half-blind woman carrying a baby on her back.

The old man said, "Let me tell you what I can. The girl lives close by, near your inn. Come, I will show you."

Wei could not believe his good fortune!

After hearing the news, Wei wanted to know about his wife-to-be: "Where is she then?" he asked. "What kind of family is she from?" He wanted to know everything.

The old man took some red thread from his bag. "You see," he said, "this thread is used to link a couple's feet together when they are born. No matter how far apart they may live, how different their social status—even if their families are enemies —a man and woman will eventually marry if their feet are tied together with this red thread."

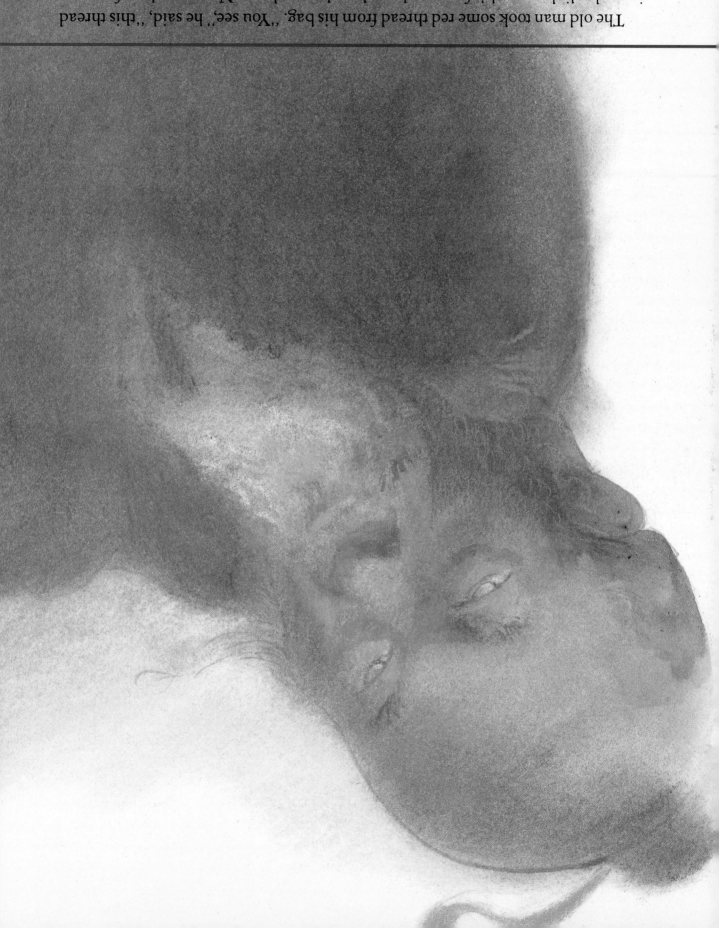

"Let me see . . ." the old man said, looking in his book. "No, General Pan's daughter is of a higher status than you, but even if she were not, you are not supposed to marry her." His finger stopped on the page. "Here. Your wife is only three years old now. You won't marry her for fourteen years."

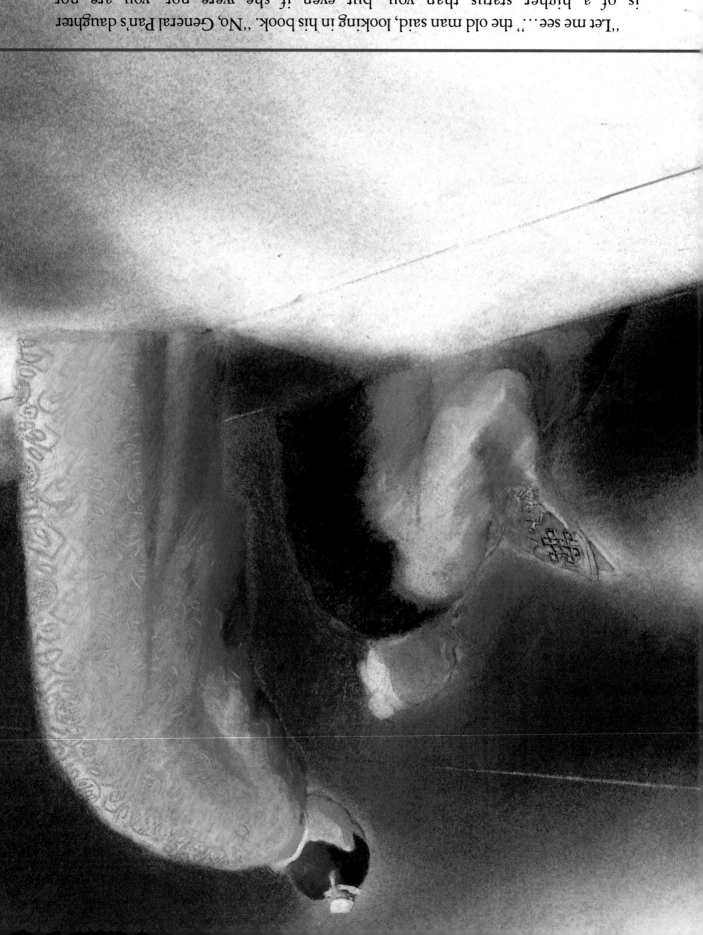

"Then what is your business?"

"Marriage," the old man answered.

"This is wonderful!" Wei said. "In ten years I have had no luck in finding a wife. I have come to see if I might marry General Pan's daughter. Perhaps you can tell me if this time I will have a little luck."

Finally, the old man said slowly, "It is not a book from this world." Wei was surprised. "If you are from a spirit world, why are you here?" Now the old man smiled. "We spirits have some affairs here, so we travel between the two worlds. Today you have come early and caught me between them."

"What language is this you are reading, uncle," Wei asked, "and what kind of book is that?"

At first the old man didn't answer.

"Uncle?" Still Wei got no reply from the old man. "Uncle!"

As Wei drew close, he could see that the old man was paging through a big book. Curious, Wei came closer and was surprised to see strange character-words written on the pages. They were neither Chinese nor Indian.

So eager was Wei to introduce himself to the matchmaker that he got up when the moon was still in the sky and went to the place. It was still dark when Wei saw an old man sitting before the temple with a bag at his side.

Then while on the way to Qinghe, he stayed at a small inn in Songcheng, where he heard of a matchmaker who was looking to match the daughter of General Pan, a well-known officer of the province. This matchmaker would be at the temple near the inn in the morning.

There was in Du Ling city in the province of Shensi a young man called Wei Gu, who had lost his parents when he was a mere boy. As he grew older he wanted more than anything to have a family of his own, but poor Wei Gu had no luck in finding a wife.

To the time given freely, unsaid,
   the ground crossed and crossed again, unknown,
   and the virtuous influences, undetected.

                                        E. Y.

Copyright © 1993 by Ed Young

Philomel Books, a division of The Putnam & Grosset Group,

200 Madison Avenue, New York, NY 10016.

Printed in Hong Kong by South China Printing Co. (1988), Ltd.

Book design by Nanette Stevenson. Lettering by David Gatti.

The text is set in Garamond #3.

The artist used watercolor and pastel to create the

illustrations for this book.

Library of Congress Cataloging-in-Publication Data

Young, Ed.   Red thread / by Ed Young.   p.   cm.

Summary: Early one morning Wei Gu meets an old man

from the spirit world who tells the young bachelor

about his future bride and their life together.

[1. Folklore—China.]   I. Title.   PZ8.1.Y84Re   1993

398.21′0951—dc20

[E]   91-45442   CIP   AC

ISBN 0-399-21969-2

1 3 5 7 9 10 8 6 4 2

First Impression